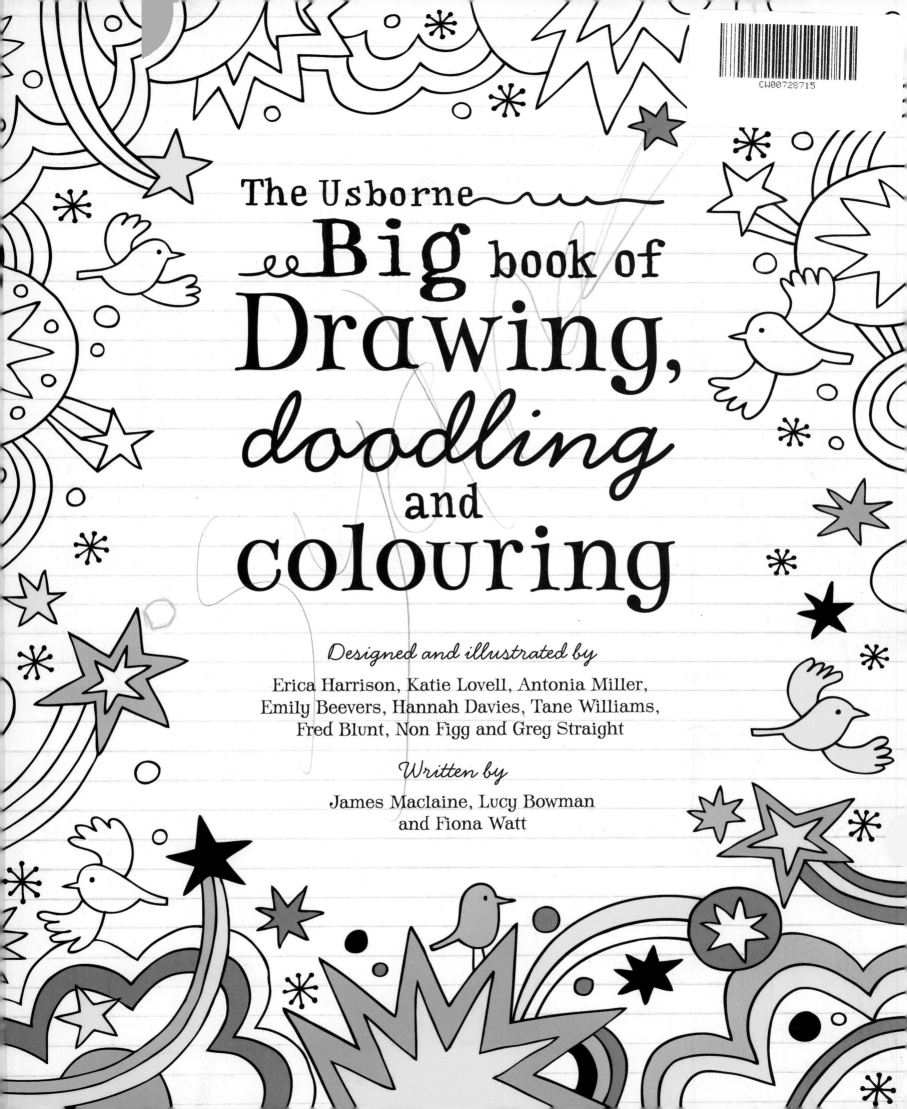

The Usborne
Big book of
Drawing,
doodling
and
colouring

Designed and illustrated by

Erica Harrison, Katie Lovell, Antonia Miller,
Emily Beevers, Hannah Davies, Tane Williams,
Fred Blunt, Non Figg and Greg Straight

Written by

James Maclaine, Lucy Bowman
and Fiona Watt

How to use this book...

On some of the pages you'll find ideas for what to do, but you can do whatever you like.

Use pens, pencils or crayons to complete the pictures.

You could fill in large areas, or add stripes, spots or patterns of your own.

When you draw on top of a shape with a pen, wait for a couple of seconds for the ink to dry, so that it doesn't smudge.

Fill the page with a pattern of shapes.

Copy these shapes or design your own.

Draw different faces on these animal heads.

Doodle a hairy-legged spider dangling from each thread.

Add some flies stuck to the web, too.

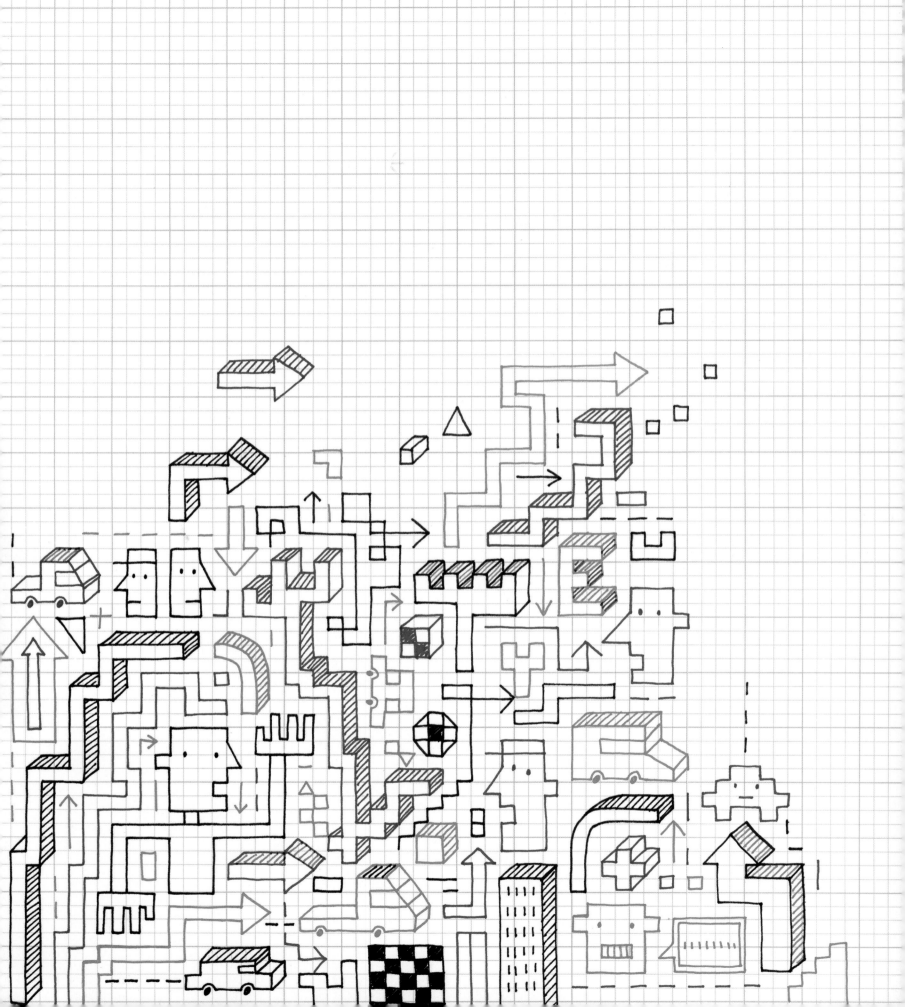

Use the grid lines to draw lots of doodles.

Fill the gaps with swirly patterns.

Doodle bright patterns on the fish.

Create a city.

Doodle more branches.

Doodle more birds.

Doodle more flowers.

Turn these shapes into monsters.

Doodle action stickmen...

...fighting...

...diving...

...kicking...

...or climbing.

Draw more partying penguins.

Fill in the snakes with different patterns.

Hissss

HISS

Draw your own
snakes on this page.

Add lots of patterns to the buildings and roofs.

Fill the page with zigzag patterns.

Doodle lots more bright
toadstools sprouting up.

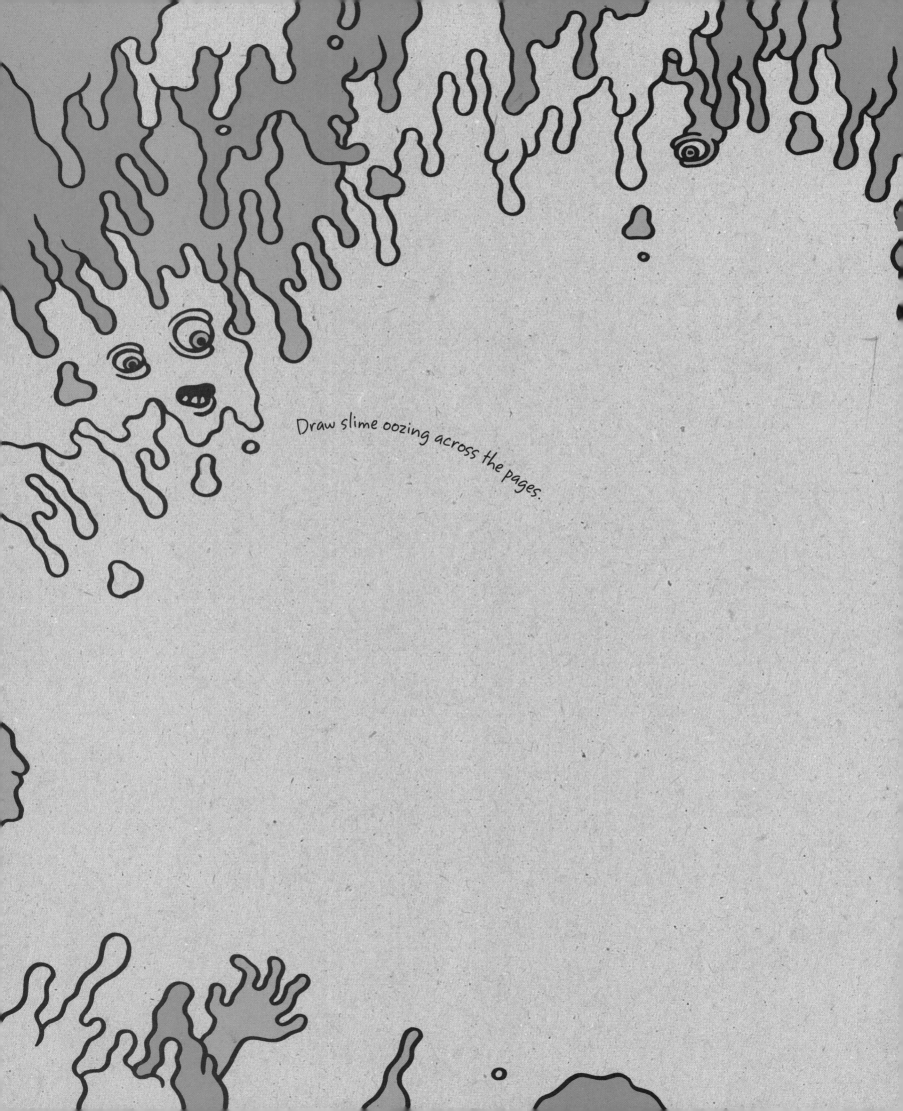

Draw slime oozing across the pages.

Add bulging eyes and toothy mouths to create some slime monsters, too.

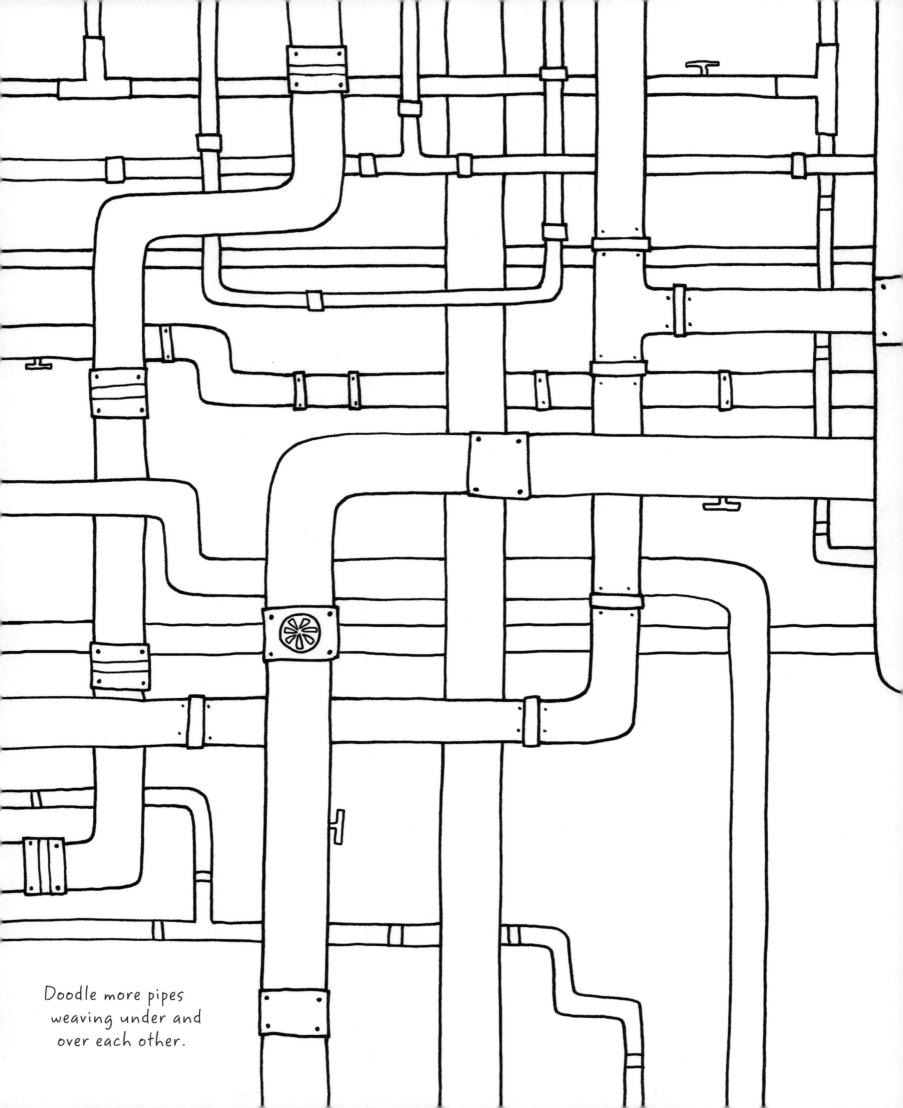

Doodle more pipes weaving under and over each other.

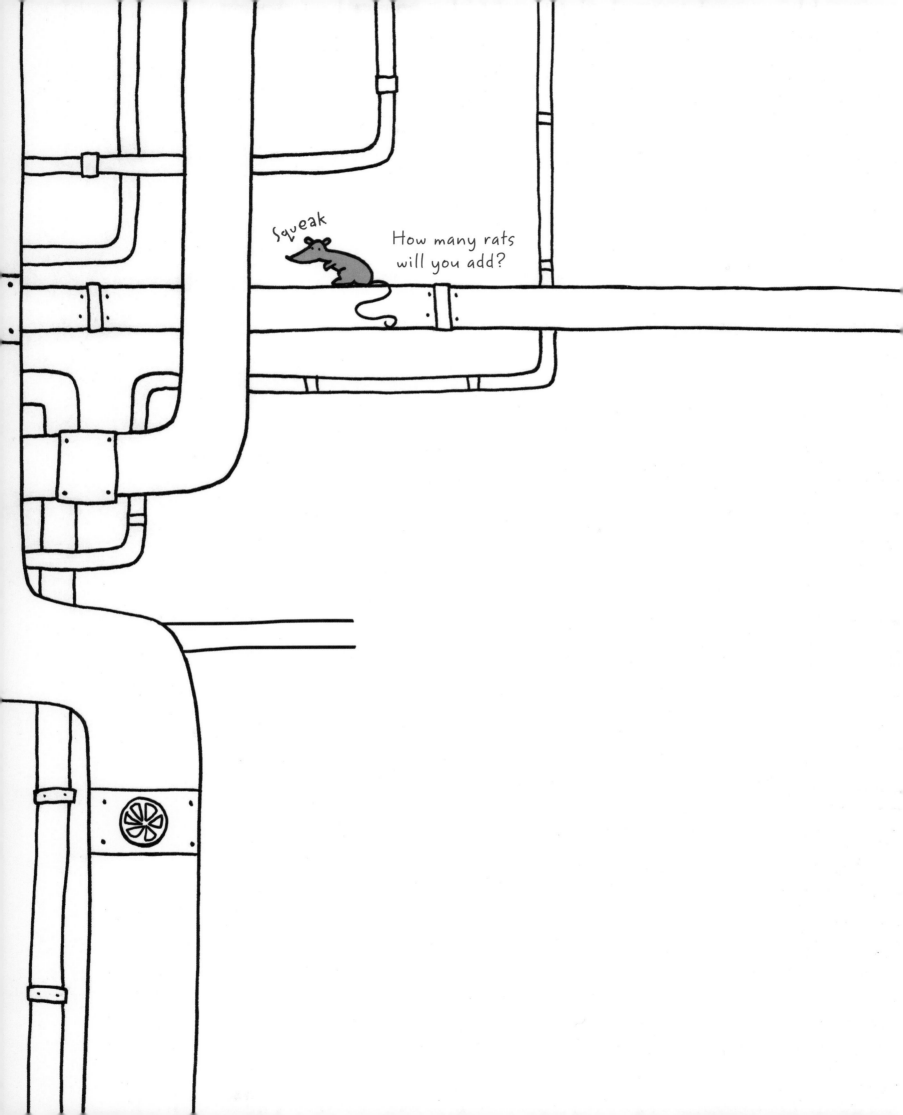

Draw lots of flowers.

Add some busy bugs, too.

Buzzzzz

Finish the trees, and add more birds and footprints in the snow.

Fill the window with cupcakes, pastries and cakes.

OPEN

Shop hours Mon-Sat 9am-6pm

Fill in some of the shapes.

FLASH

Make the audience even bigger.

Who is holding this camera?

ugh ugh

chirp

Scribble lots of fur on the woolly mammoths. Give the figures hair, beards and hairy clothes.

Draw in the missing faces. Can you completely fill the pages with ghosts?

Whoooo

Ooo

Boo

Turn each shape into a different person.

Continue this pattern without
taking your pen off the paper.

Draw more houses, trees, bushes and fences.

Doodle lots and lots of buttons until there is room for no more.

Doodle red patterns on the doves.

Using the triangles as a guide, take lines for a walk across this page...

...and down this side.

Fill the pages with patterned bugs.

Doodle clouds, stars, planets and birds.

Try filling in this flowery pattern with lots of different pencils.

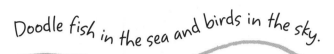

Doodle fish in the sea and birds in the sky.

Join the shapes with doodled patterns.

Complete the robots below, then draw your own too.

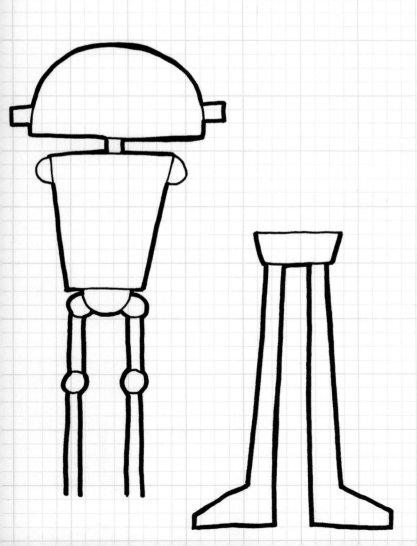

How many different outfits can you design?

Doodle patterns on these bicycles with a black pen.

Scribble with these pens and pencils.

Draw long-tongued frogs and hovering flies.

slurp!

Fill the page with bright,
patterned circles.

Draw lots of people skiing down the snowy slope.

ZOOOM

Doops

Wooooo

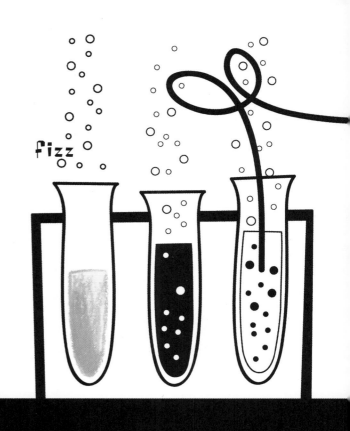

gurgle

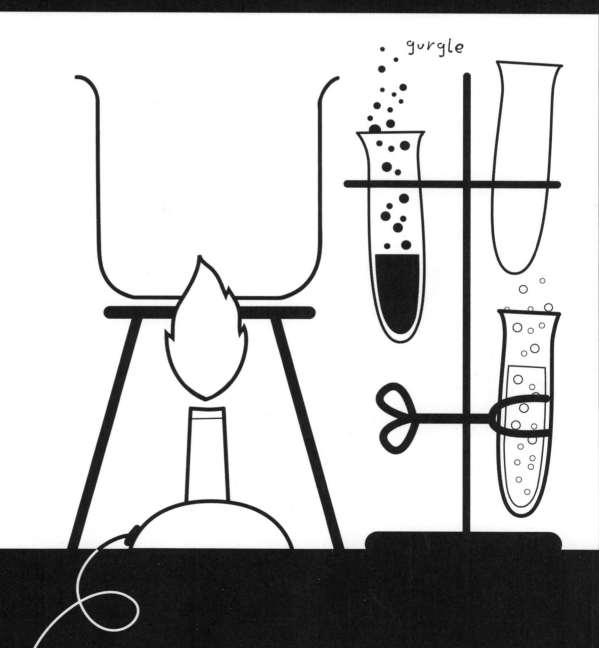

ooh
ooh

ahh
ahh

Draw monkeys playing on the branches.

Keep doodling triangles, patterns and trucks until you can doodle no more.

Doodle butterflies fluttering across the pages.

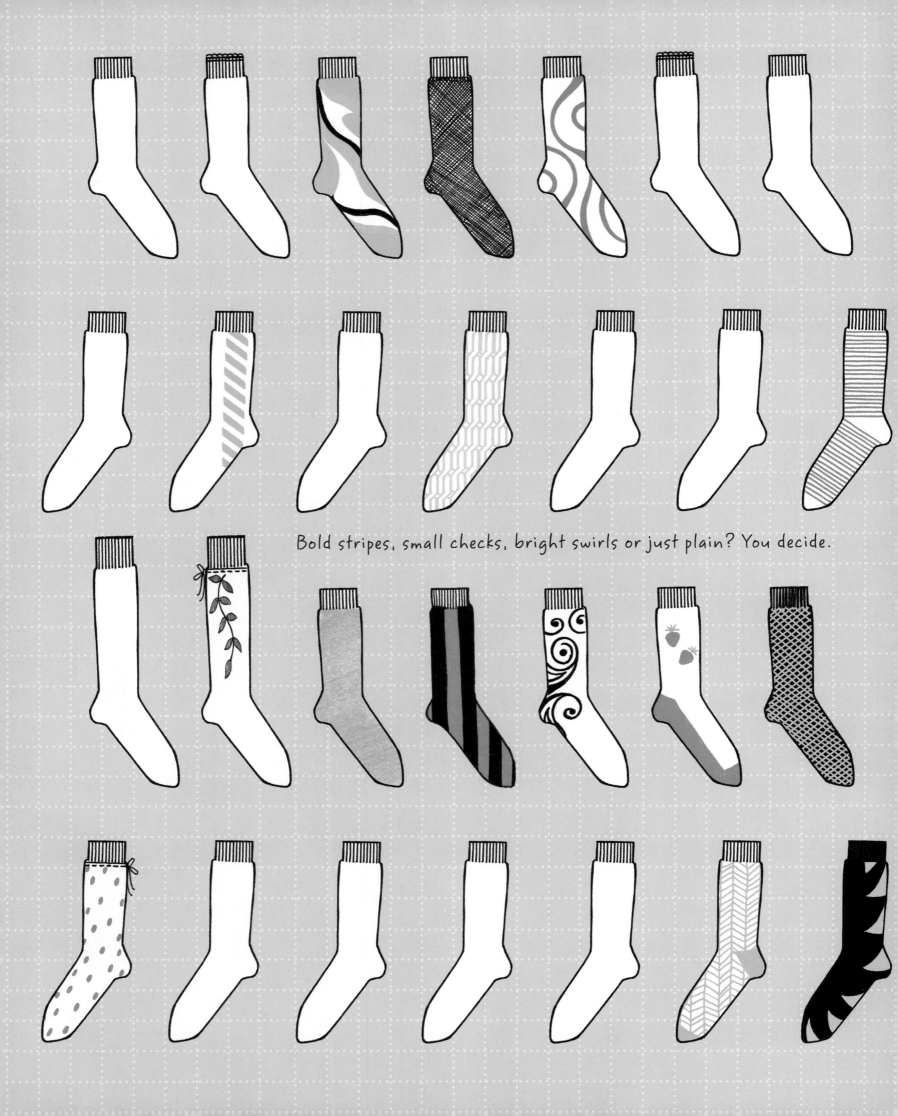

Bold stripes, small checks, bright swirls or just plain? You decide.

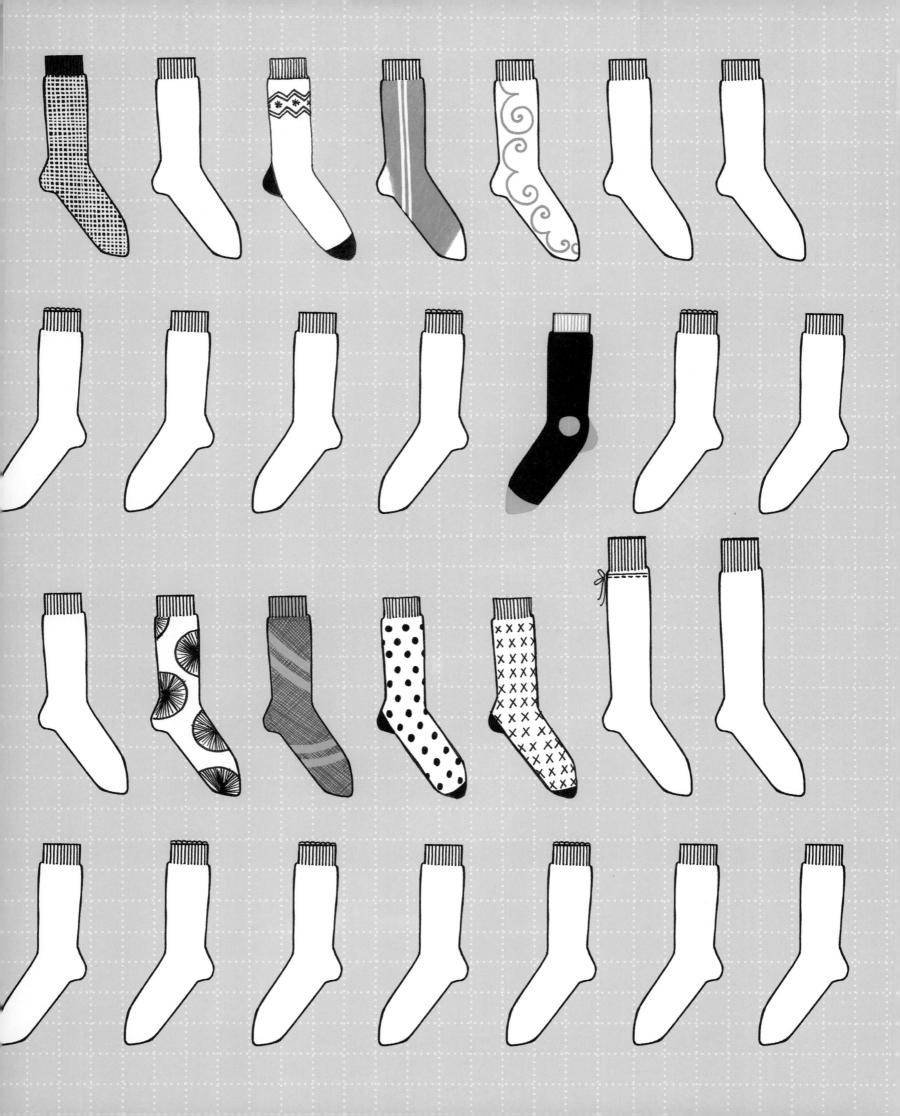

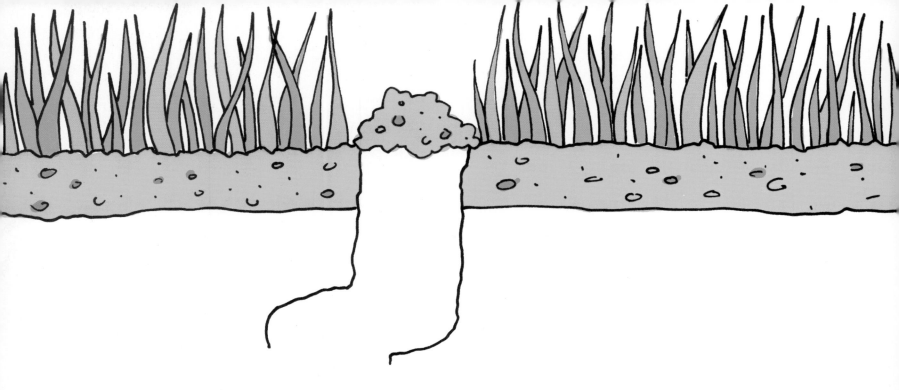

What's buried under the ground?

Fill this side with hearts...

...and this side with stars.

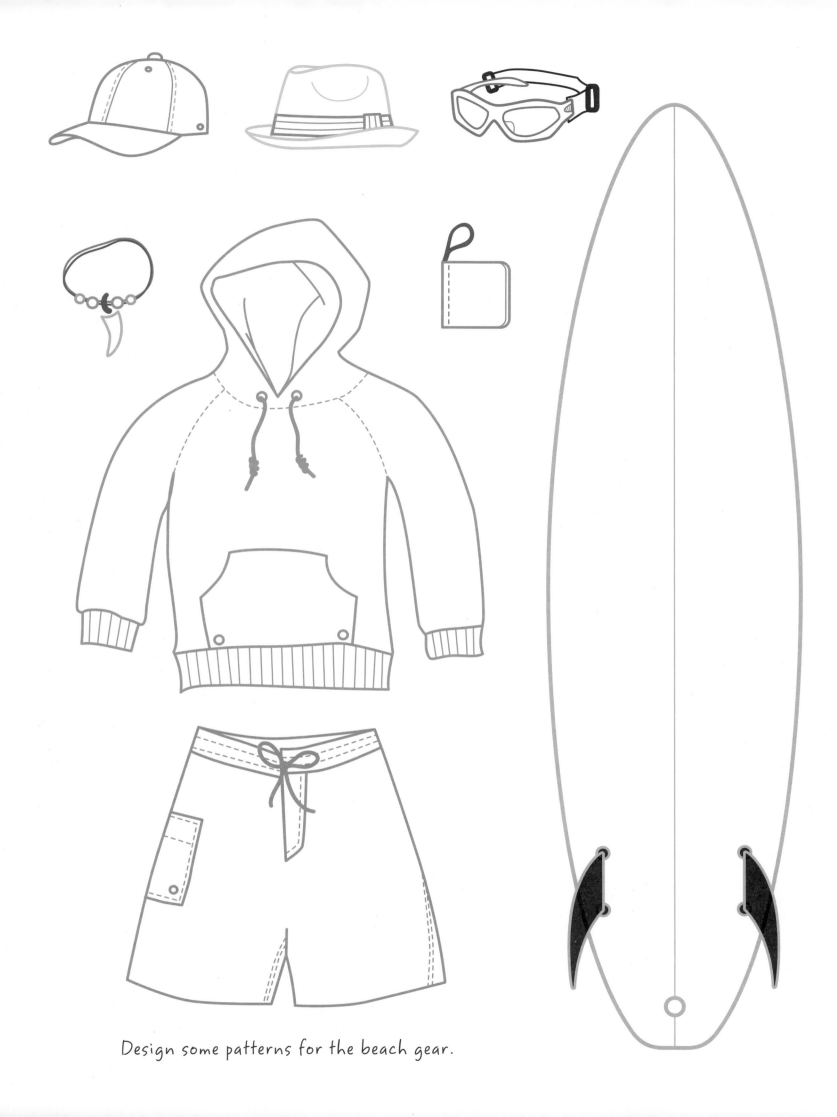

Design some patterns for the beach gear.

How many greens and yellows do you have? Use them to fill in the forest.

Draw some whales and
doodle lots of waves.

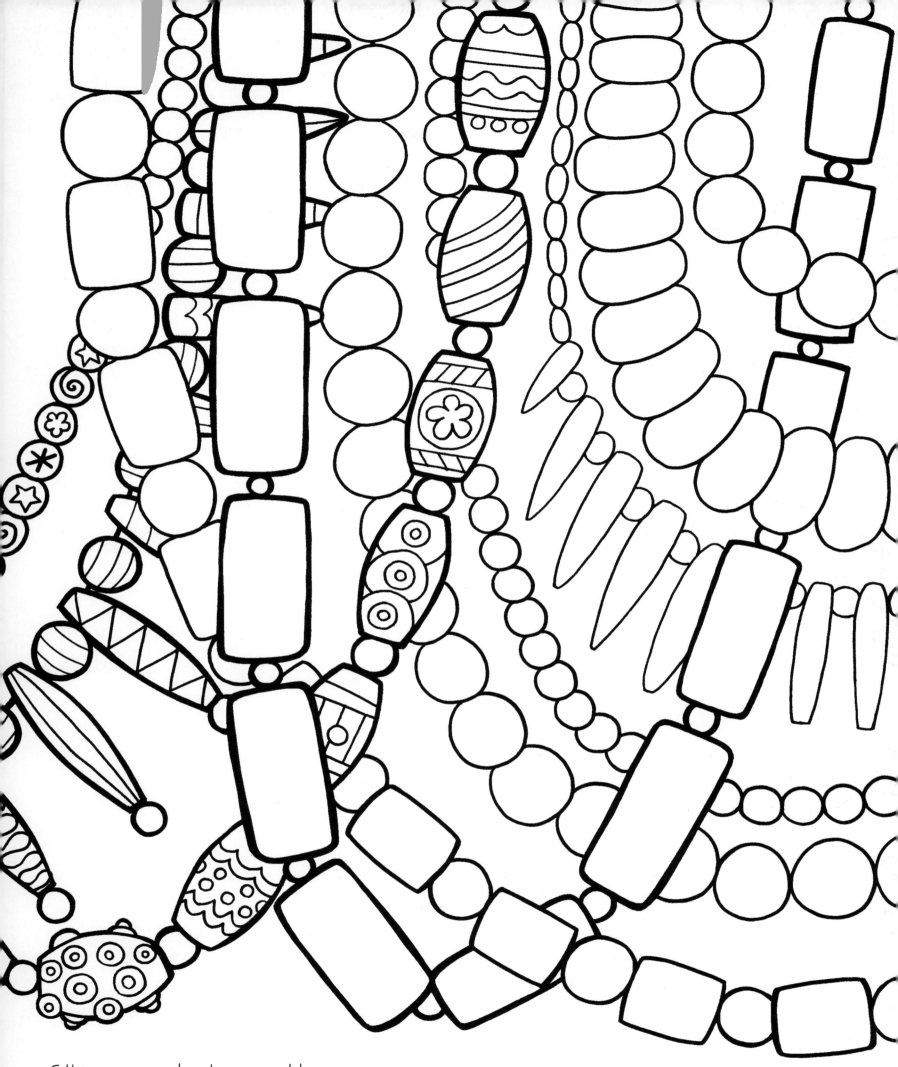

Fill in as many beads as you like.

Monsters marching across the pages...

Doodle flowers, flowers and more flowers.

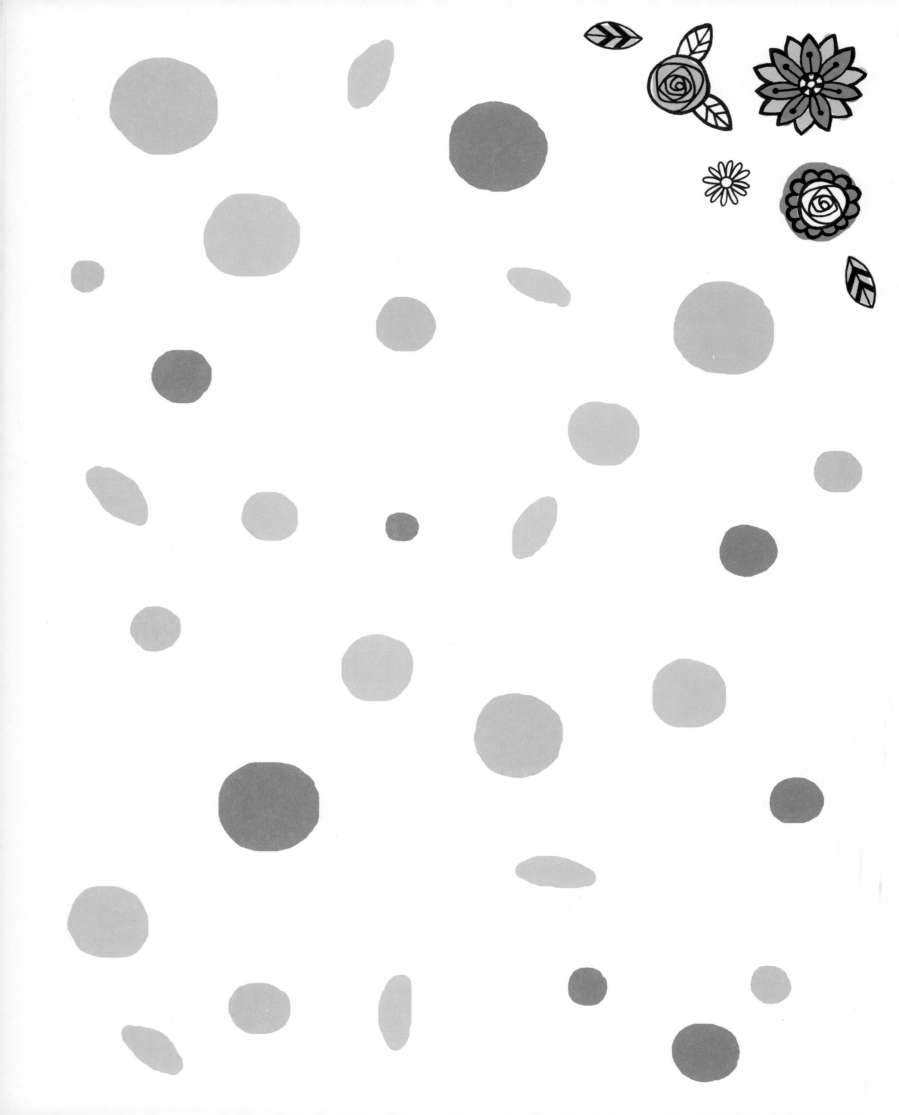

Draw faces and patterns on these owls.

Some bats are flying; others are hanging in the trees.

Doodle big and small flowers, and insects flying around.

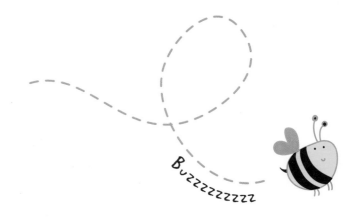

Buzzzzzzzzz

Turn the shapes into monsters attacking a city.
Then, doodle vehicles and people fighting back.

BOOM...

Copy the lacy patterns onto the unfinished squares or design some new ones of your own.

Can you complete the circuit board? Add circles, squares and lines, and any other shapes you like.

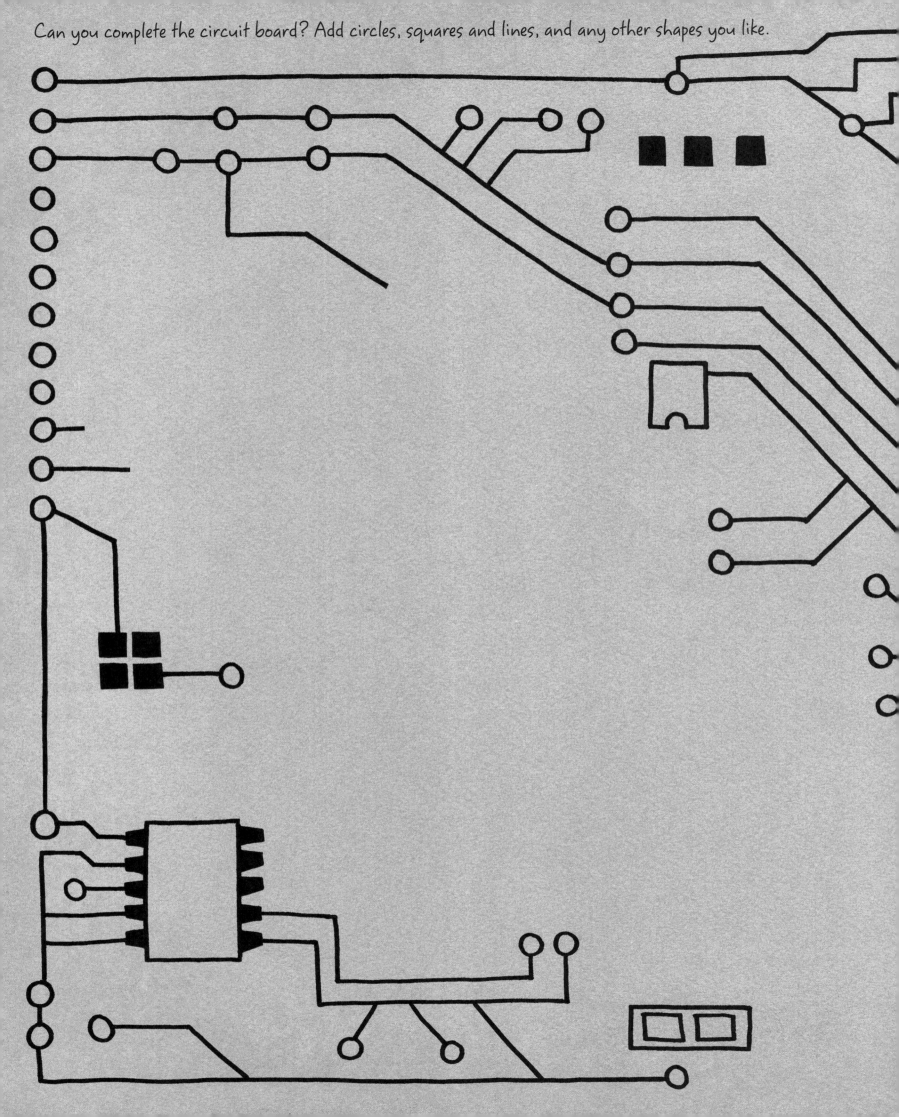

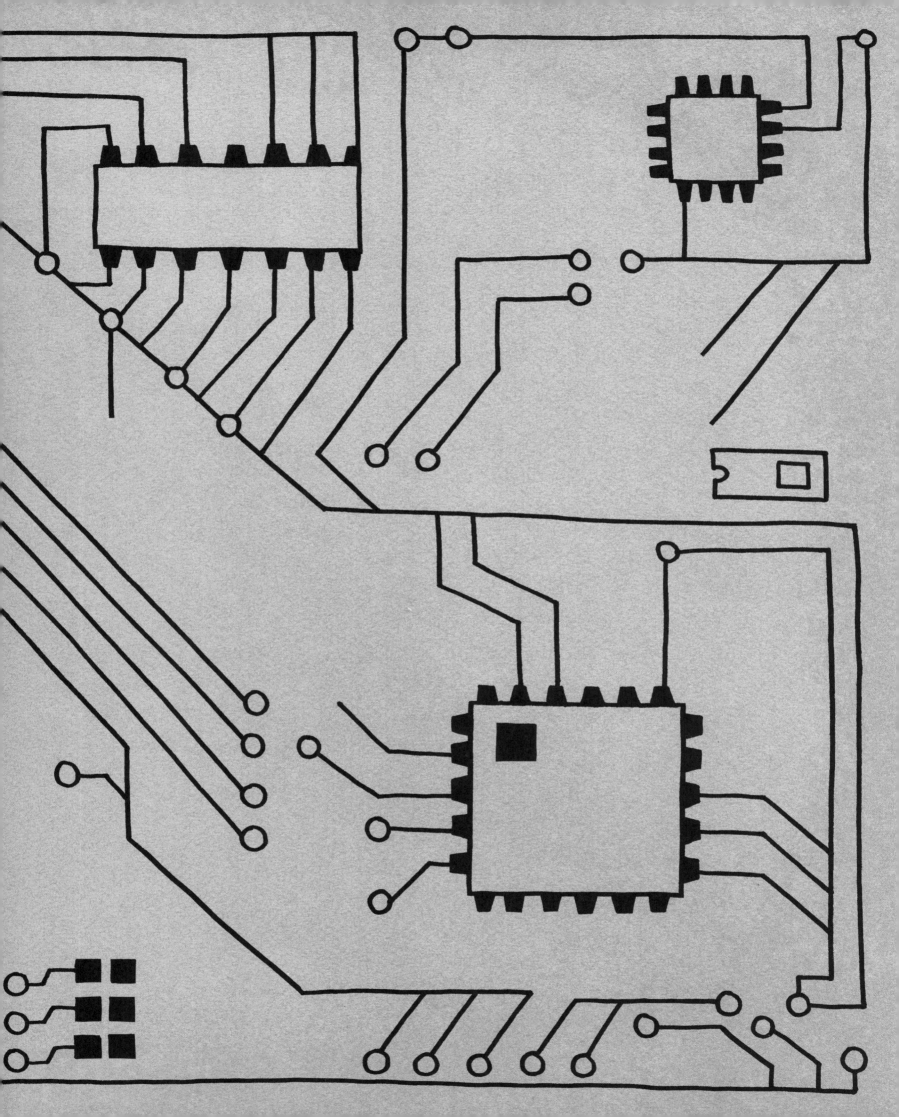

Sketch more jumping horses.

wow

Put more presents on the pile, then decorate them.

Prickly cacti and slithering snakes...

SSSSSSS

Doodle patterns on these snowflakes.

Finish these rows of houses.

Add doors, windows and decorations. Who do you think lives inside?

Turn these shapes into faces.

Maybe give some of them names?

Ivan

Ali

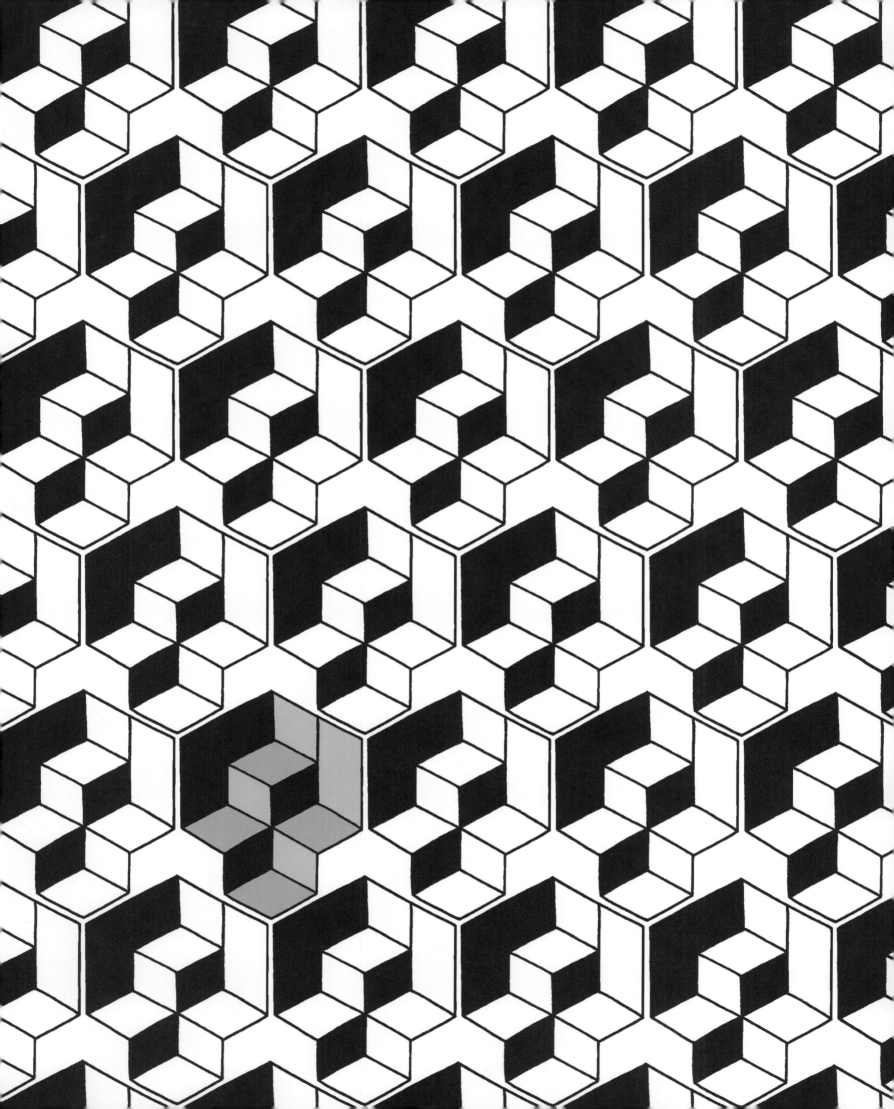

Add ghosts, monsters and ladders to the different levels.

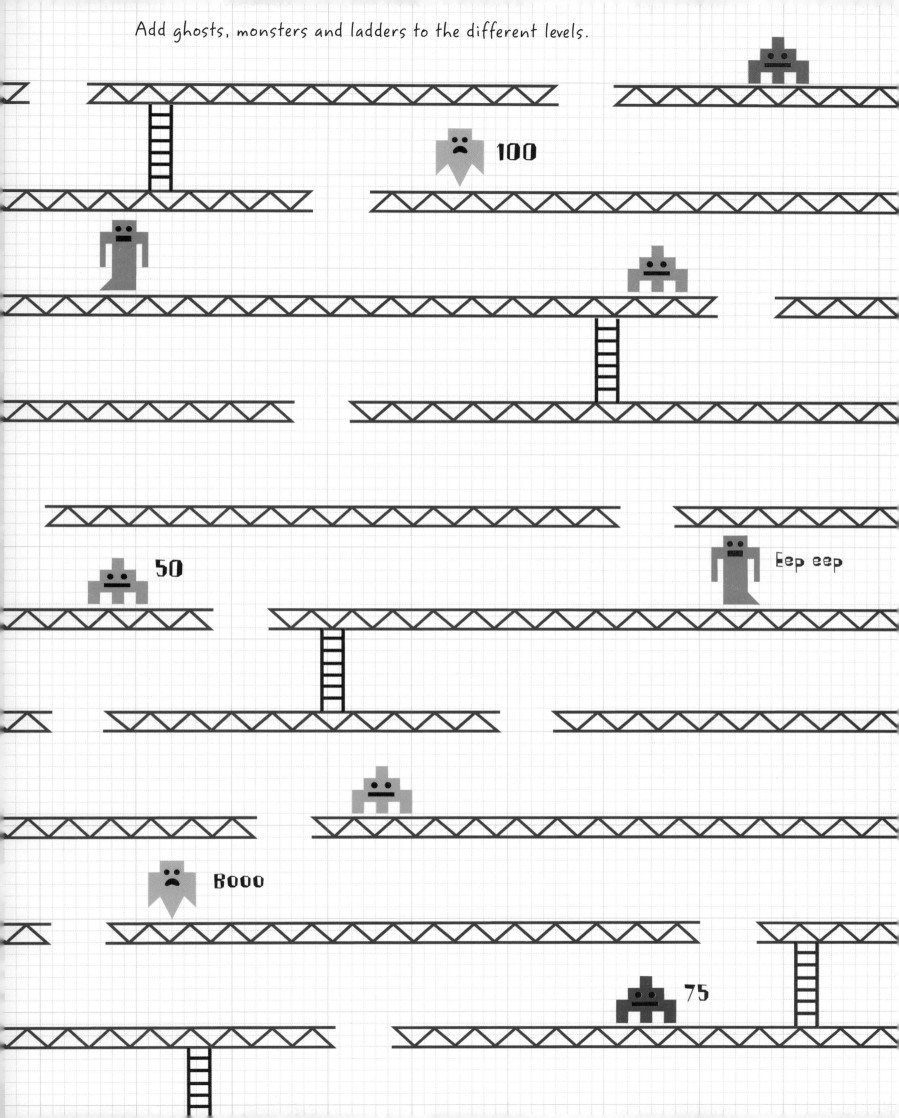

100

50

Eep eep

Booo

75

Roses, roses everywhere...fill the pages with more.

Use a black pen to fill the pages with bugs, ants and other creepy crawlies.

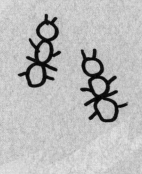

It's a sunny day, so fill the washing line with clothes.

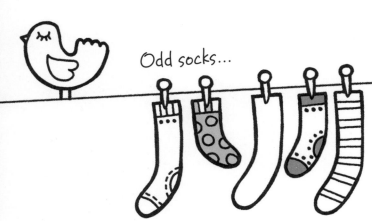

Odd socks...

Make them pairs.

Decorate the snails' shells and add some slimy trails.

Draw UFOs in red and fighter space jets in blue.

Doodle more lanes and vehicles to create a traffic jam.

Turn these shapes into snowmen.

Doodle cages for
the songbirds.

Draw an alien inside each flying saucer.

Draw fish in the sea and stars in the sky.

Design the buildings, then fill the streets with shoppers.

Continue doodling monsters without taking your pen off the paper.

Turn these fingerprints into different faces.

Happy...

...sleepy...

...angry...

...or scared.

Give these plants eyes, teeth and mouths.
Then, add lots of flies about to be trapped.

Bzz Bzz Bzz

Turn these shapes into tigers with stripes, claws and teeth.

GRRr

Add scribbly manes to these lions, too.

RAA

ROARR

Doodle patterns and fill in the shapes.

Draw in the missing snowballs,
then fill in the picture.

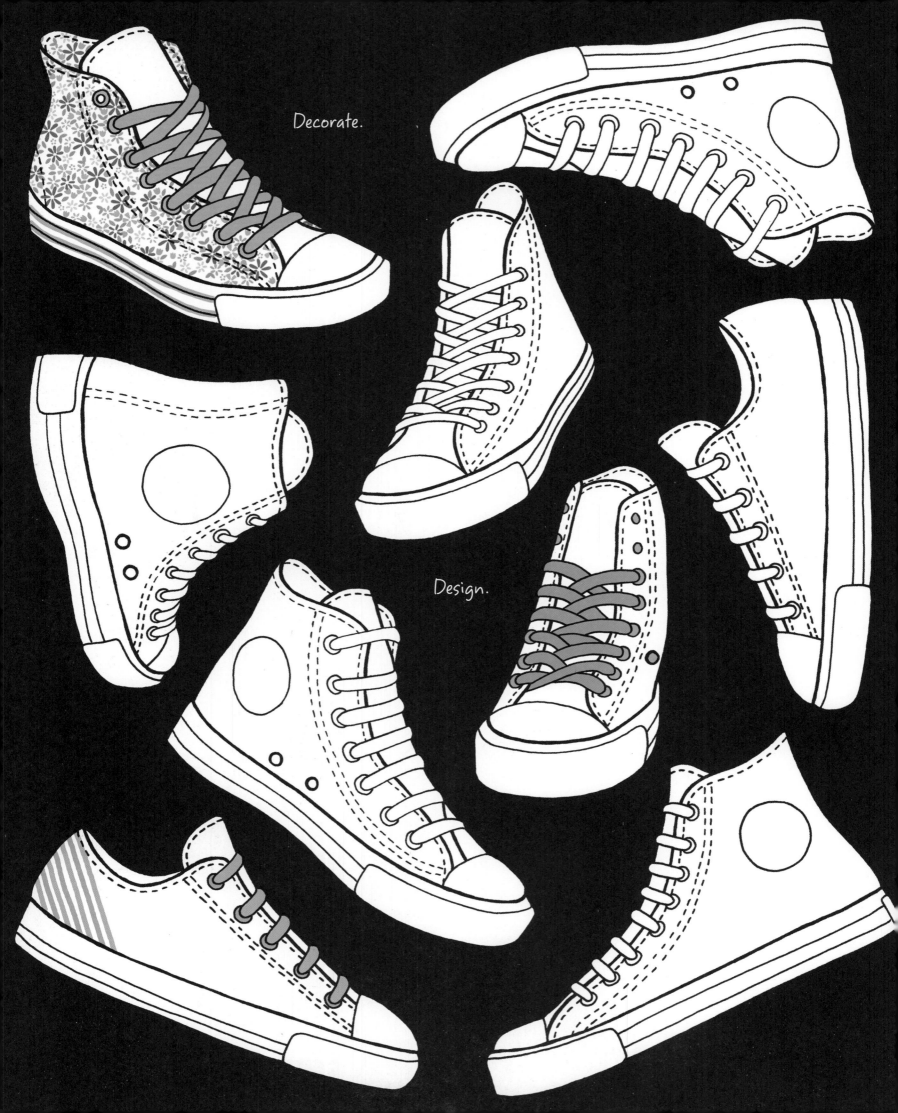

Decorate.

Design.

Customize.

Finish this swarm of bees.

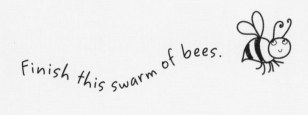

buzzz

buzz

bzzz

Create a dinosaur landscape.

Doodle black fish swimming in the sea.

Add some coral and seaweed too.

Fill the trees with doodled leaves.

Fill in this crazy machine.

Doodle faces and bodies on these numbers...

3 0 0 1 6

9 7 4

5 1 3 8

8 4 2

7 0 5

You called?

Decorate the Russian matryoshka dolls.

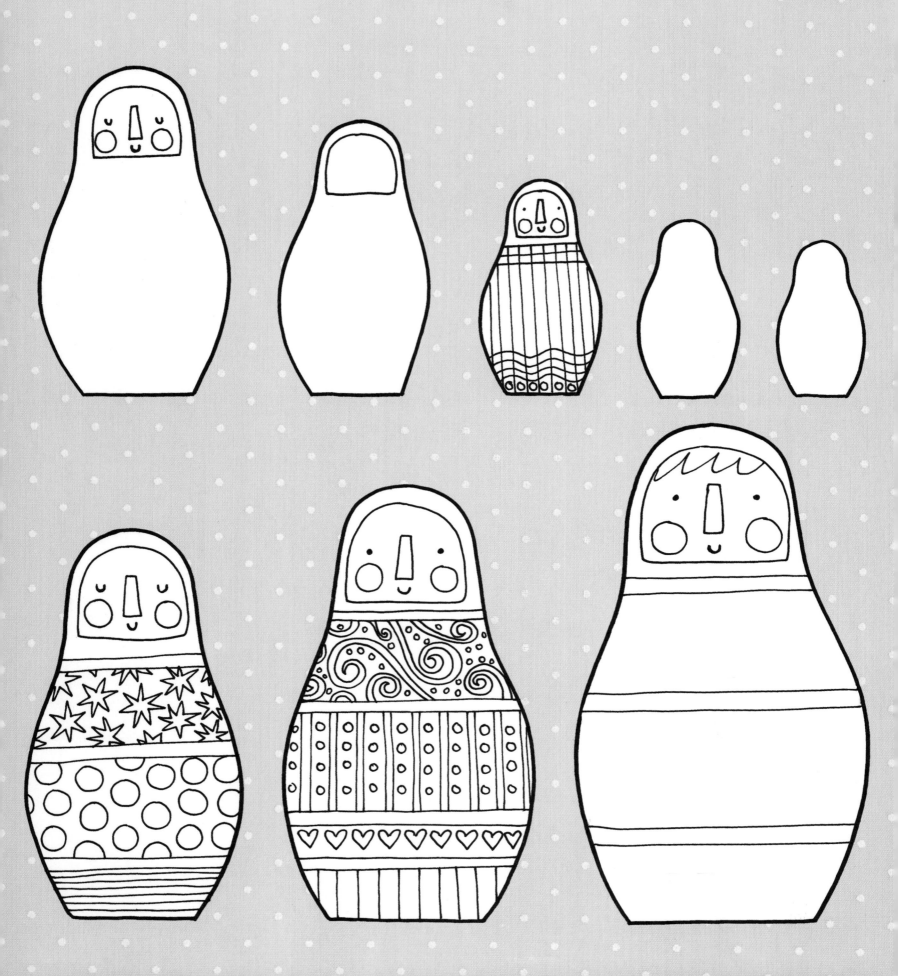

ta-da

Give these strongmen
weights to lift.

Add faces to the crowd.

Doodle patterns on their leotards, too.

ugggh

Doodle lots of bright lights along the wires.

Finish the buildings, too.

Doodle angry faces on the clouds and raindrops.

BOOM

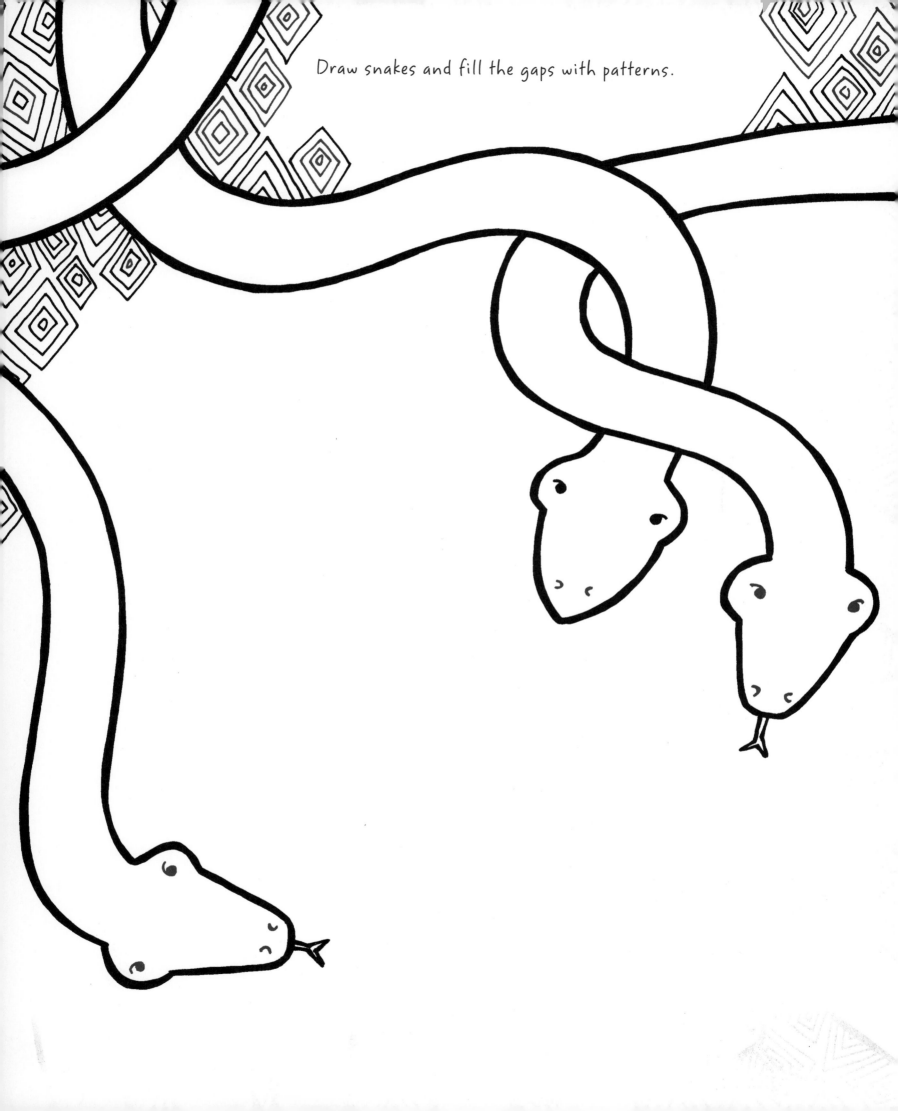

Draw snakes and fill the gaps with patterns.

Keep on doodling without taking your pen off the paper.
Doodle up, down, left, right, round and round...

When in Rome, doodle as the Romans do.

Turn the shapes into arches...

...columns...

...and temples, too.

Fill the fishing boat's net with its catch.

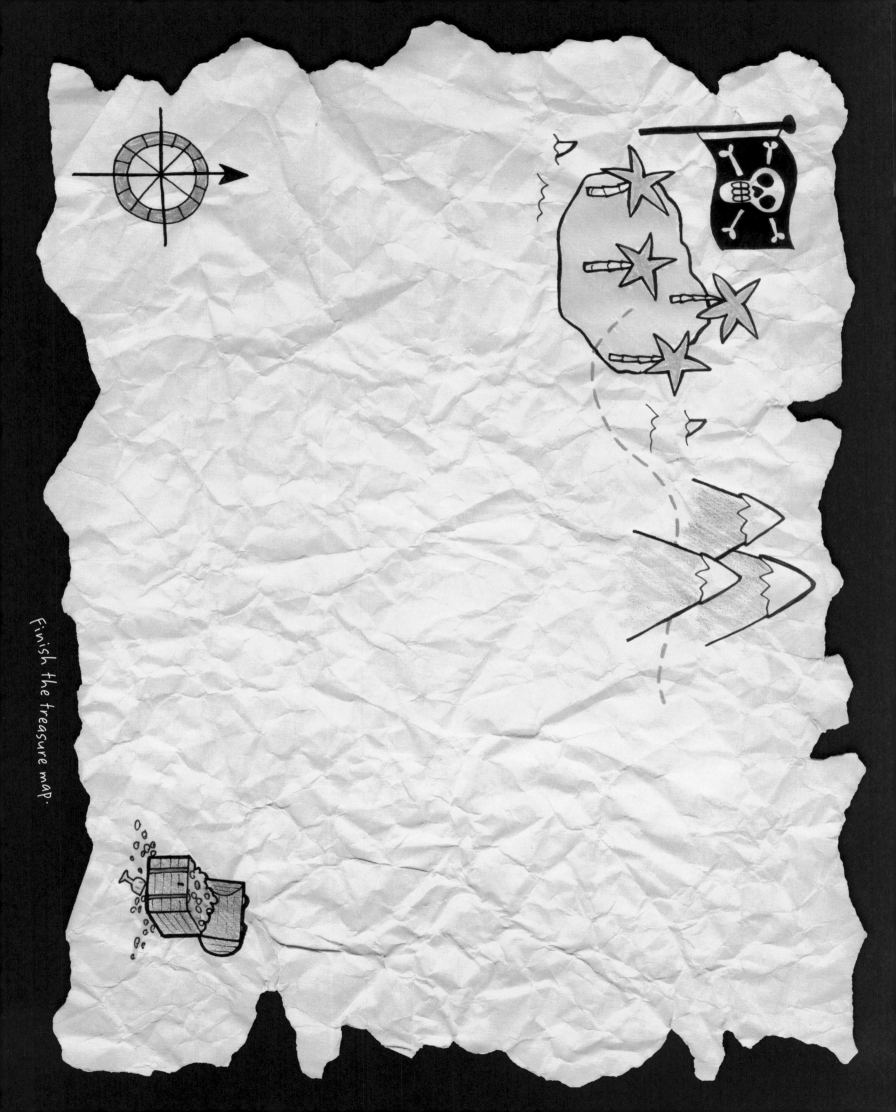

Finish the treasure map.

Draw pointed teeth...

...and add lots of scales.

Doodle patterns on these fantastic flamingoes.

Who said they all had to be pink?

Doodle some greedy mice...

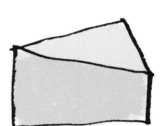

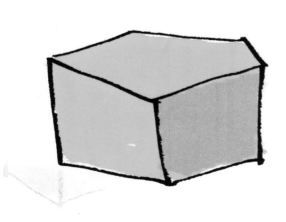

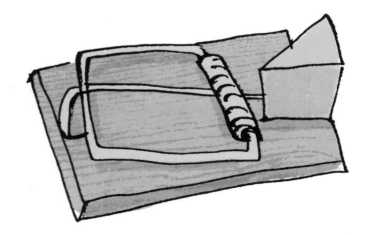

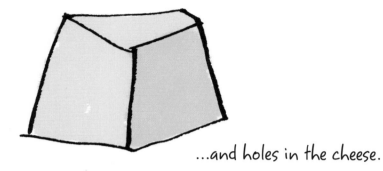

...and holes in the cheese.

DAVE'S BRAIN

Draw some more gruesome things in the jars...

...and label them.

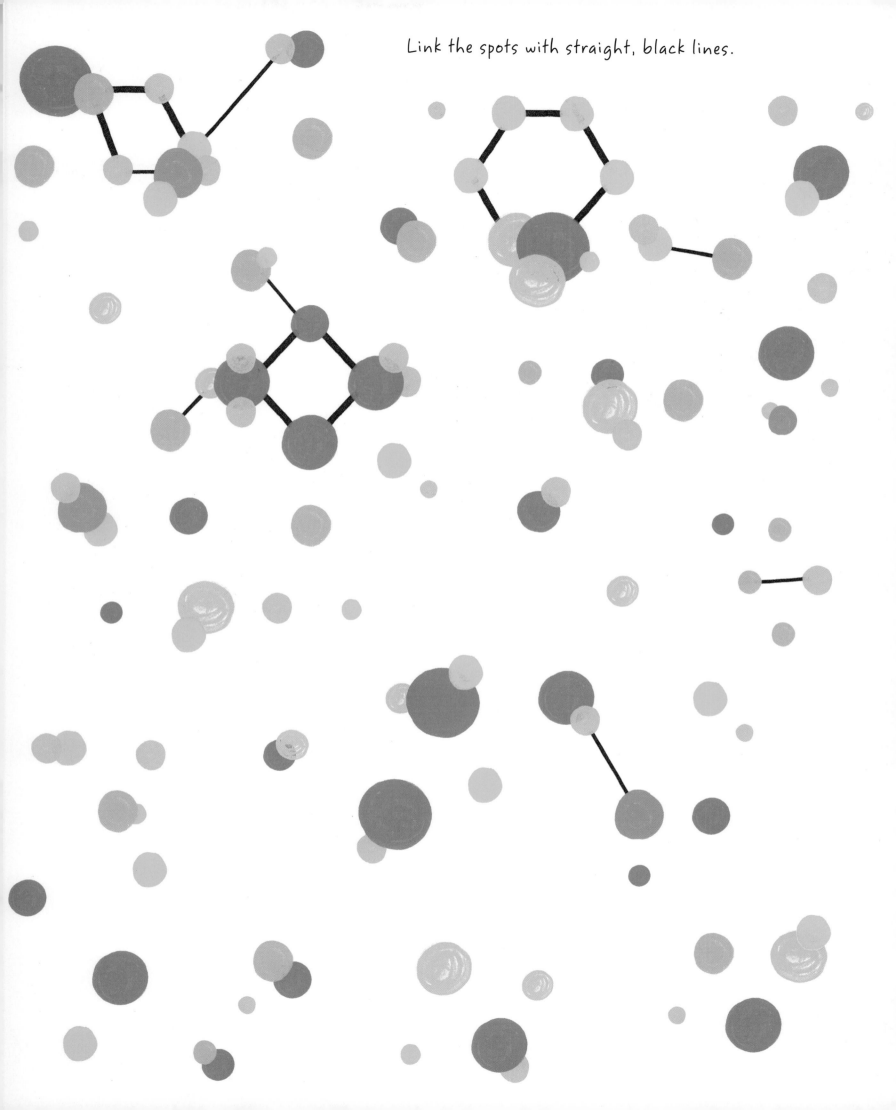

Link the spots with straight, black lines.

Add more houses and trees to
make the snowy village bigger.

Fill these winding roads with cars and trucks.

Design the figures' clothes.

Turn each spot into a different face.

Hello

My name's Boris

Maybe add hair, a bow tie or a hat?

Draw flowers in the empty vases...

...and decorate them, too.

Turn these shapes into cogs.

Connect some with belts, too.

Doodle patterns on
the shells.

Find your red and black pens, and continue this doodle...

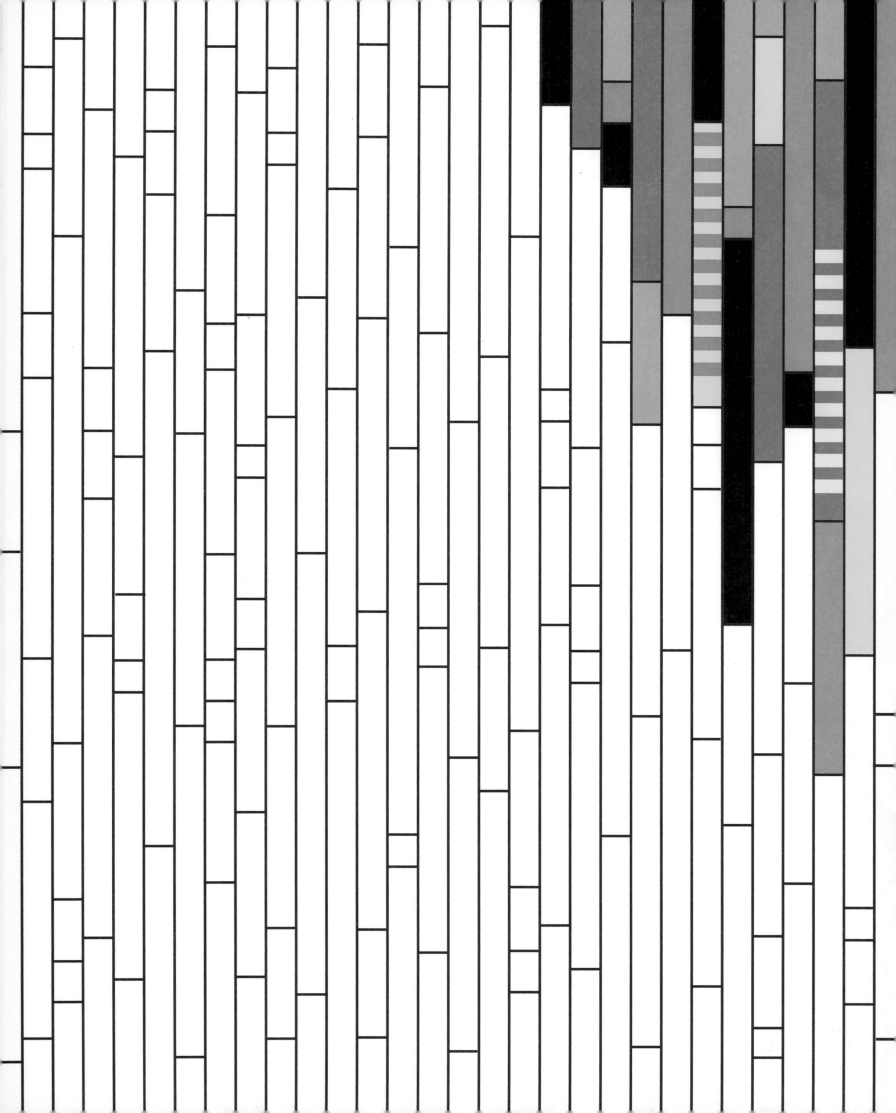

Turn these shapes into bugs.

Paisley patterns for you to fill...

Draw sea creatures frightened by
the giant octopus...

...and doodle suckers on its tentacles.

Fill these boxes with whatever you like.

Complete the skyscrapers and doodle lots more.

Turn these shapes into fire-breathing dragons.

Add lots of scales, horns and scary teeth.

First published in 2013 by Usborne Publishing Ltd., Usborne House, 83-85 Saffron Hill, London ECIN 8RT, England.
www.usborne.com © 2013, 2012, 2010 Usborne Publishing Ltd. The name Usborne and the devices ♀ ⊕ are Trade Marks
of Usborne Publishing Ltd. All rights reserved. No part of this publication may be reproduced, stored in a retrieval system or
transmitted in any form or by any means, electronic, mechanical, photocopying, recording or otherwise without the
prior permission of the publisher. UE. First published in America in 2013.